HUGH CONWAY

Capital Wine

Contents

A Very Short Introduction	1
Capital Wine	2
At What Cost	16
VERY SHORT CLASSICS	33

A Very Short Introduction

Hugh Conway is the pen name of Frederick John Fargus.

Fargus was born in Bristol in 1847, the son of an auctioneer. Although he originally intended to enter his father's business he had a brief dalliance with the sea, almost joining the navy as a trainee officer, before agreeing to return to Bristol where he worked as an accountancy clerk until his father's death in 1868, whereupon he took over the family auction house.

During his time as a clerk he had written the lyrics to a number of songs using the name Hugh Conway and, encouraged by the Bristol publisher James William Arrowsmith, he turned his hand to stories and novels. His first novella, a thriller entitled *Called Back*, was a huge success, selling 350,000 copies and enlisting fans including Emily Dickinson.

In 1885, following a bout of ill health, Fargus went to the French Riviera where he caught typhoid fever and died at the age of only 37. Several of his books and stories were published posthumously, including the two included in this volume.

Capital Wine

"Capital wine, John," I said, holding the glass between the lamp and my eyes, and admiring the rich, ruby tint.

"Capital, isn't it?" replied John, cuddling his glass in the palm of his hand in order to warm the wine and fully bring out its bouquet and flavour.

We had just finished the sort of dinner I consider perfection for two persons. A drop of clear soup, a sole and a brace of woodcocks. That is, to my mind, as nice a dinner as can be devised, and one which, having eaten, you have no occasion to reproach yourself with high feeding or gluttony. Others may devour huge cuts from sirloin, leg or saddle, but I am always contented with a humble menu like the above.

"Thirty-four, of course," I said, after tasting the port again.

John nodded and continued nursing his glass.

"Where did you buy it, John?" I inquired.

"Didn't buy it," replied John. "You can't buy such wine as that now."

"A gift from a grateful client, I presume," I said, re-filling my glass.

"Not a bit of it, clients ain't so generous, nowadays. If we can get our costs we are content."

"Well, how did you get it?"

"Stole it," replied John, shortly.

"What do you mean?"

"I mean, I stole that wine as much as ever a thief stole a watch. I planned, plotted, and at last succeeded in effecting the theft. You would have done the same, would you not?"

"I don't know. It depends upon the risk of conviction and imprisonment. But, tell me all about it."

John placed all the bottles fairly between us, and began:—

"You know my old uncle, William Slagg—at any rate you have heard of him. Well, he made a good bit of money drysalting, and, what is more, made it when he was a youngish man. He must have been well brought up, or mixed with the right sort of people, for he developed a wonderful taste for wine, and, instead of doing what lots of people do now, more shame to them—send out to their grocer's for half-a-dozen as they want it—used to buy a pipe or a butt at a time and lay it down. He reaped the reward of his sensible conduct for, when he retired from drysalting, he found himself with a cellar not only amply stocked, but without a drop of bad wine in it. So he settled down to live comfortably on his investments, and to drink his wine in peace.

"Poor old boy! It was beautiful to see him and amusing to hear him with the decanters in front of him. He knew the history of each wine he gave you, and nearly all had a tender reminiscence for him. He would sip a drop of sherry, and look across at me, and say: 'I call this more than wine, John. It is a poem; something to enjoy and think over.' Then he would turn to the port. 'I bought that pipe, John, when I made a wonderful hit in tallow;' or 'that claret, John, I laid down when log-wood went up to such a price,' and so on.

"The old man was by no means a wine-bibber, but he would take his four or five glasses after dinner and enjoy them. He suffered a little from gout before he died, but not more than many elderly gentlemen with rubicund faces. He lived a good many years enjoying the fruit of his labours and the juice in his cellars, and at last slipped away quietly and peacefully. His last words were to me:—

"'Give them the '47 and the green seal sherry at the funeral, John. There's more body, more solemnity in those wines than some of the others.'

"And then old William Slagg went off, and I have no doubt is now the best judge of nectar in the upper regions.

"He left me his executor, and, I am happy to say, the reversion of a considerable sum when his widow dies.

"But it was not without a feeling of disappointment I found all the contents of his house, including the cellar of wines, were hers absolutely.

"It seemed absurd for a splendid lot of wines like that to belong to a woman who would be utterly unable to appreciate them, and whose ideas of wine were bounded, after the manner of womankind, by sweet champagne on one side and family port on the other. I had never expected to be left so much money, but had always cherished the hope that Uncle Slagg, who had greatly approved of the way in which I had discussed his liquor, would have left me those wines.

"However, I thought very likely the widow would prefer a good sum of money to the full bins, so I intended to offer to buy them after a decent interval.

"My Aunt Slagg has very different ideas to those of her late and lamented husband. I remember her, however, as a sensible woman, and having a good eye to the main chance. She had been a capital wife to William Slagg, but, about a twelvemonth before his death, she had attended some revival meetings—a lovefeast, or something of that sort—and been converted. I can't tell, of course, but I feel sure that nothing can be more annoying to an ordinary man that to find the wife of his bosom—who has jogged along with him very comfortably in a give-and-take style for many years—suddenly turn round and lecture him upon his amiable little weaknesses.

"I am convinced the shock of her conversion hastened poor old William's death. He had been so accustomed to look upon drinking good wine as the duty of a Christian, that when his wife made a new departure, and became a rabid teetotaller, the thing was too much for him, and he died trying to solve the problem. She would quote Sir Wilfred Lawson, Dr. Richardson, and other authorities, all dinner time, and, when the decanters were placed upon the table, walk away with a look of chastened sorrow upon her face. Nothing, of course, could wean Uncle Slagg from his wine-pots, as she called his little weakness, but I know after tirades, the liquor had lost some of its flavour for him, and did not taste the same as in the old days before her awakening, when she would fill his glass, and even press him to take an extra one for the sake of his health. I wonder he did not alter his will, and, no doubt, he would, had he known to what lengths her fanaticism would lead her.

"I managed, by skilful tactics, to keep on pretty good terms with the old lady. I took the temperance tracts with which she bristled, and led her to understand that, if I could not make up my mind to take the pledge at once, it was a good deal out of consideration for her husband's feelings, and I might do some day. She looked upon me as a weak vessel, but had great hopes that I might eventually be strong enough to hold the gift of grace, as she rather curiously termed it. After William Stagg's death, I had, in my position as executor, a lot of business to transact with her, and for some weeks saw her nearly every day. I thought the time was coming when I might broach the subject of the cellar to her, and, as I was walking to the house one afternoon, determined to sound her upon it, I rang and knocked for some minutes, but could get no answer to my summons. They are all upstairs, I thought, and can't hear me. Then I remembered that the day before, after going through a lot of papers of my uncle's, I had locked the drawers and put the keys in my pocket. His latch-key was amongst them, and I took the liberty of opening the door with it.

"As I entered the house, I smelt a very peculiar smell proceeding from the kitchen. It was the odour of wine and very strong. They must have broken a bottle carrying it up, I thought. Perhaps, after all, the old lady is not so strict a teetotaller when alone. And I laughed at the idea, little dreaming whence the smell came. I could find no one in any of the sitting rooms, and, as I heard persons moving in the basement, proceeded there. My Aunt, hearing my steps on the stairs, ran to the kitchen door to see who it was. I noticed she appeared vexed as she met me.

"'I am particularly engaged this afternoon, John, and can't speak to you now,' she said.

"As she spoke, I noticed the smell of the wine was almost overpowering, and I wondered what she was doing.

"She had some old gown on, and that covered with a rough, white apron, apparently soaked with some coloured fluid. She was dusty, dirty, untidy, and heated, and I noticed blood flowing from a cut on her hand. What extraordinary household exploit could she be engaged in?

"When a lady tells you decidedly she can't stop to talk to you, and when she appears up to her eyes in cleaning the house or something of that sort, the next thing to do is to make yourself scarce; so I apologised for my intrusion and promised to call again tomorrow.

"'But what a strong smell of wine, aunt?' I said. 'Don't you notice it?'

"'My servants have just broken a bottle or two,' she replied, looking rather embarrassed. 'Goodbye, John, shut the door after you.'

"'Goodbye,' I said, and retraced my steps.

"As I went up those dark kitchen stairs, a sudden thought struck me. And yet it seemed so wild and absurd that I laughed at the idea. But, before I had reached the top, it had taken full possession of me, and I felt cold and pale with dread. I could not bear the uncertainty, and determined to ascertain, at any risk, if my suspicions were correct. Instead, therefore, of shutting the door from the outside, I shut it with a good bang from the inside and waited, scarcely breathing, at the top of the stairs. After a minute's listening, my ears caught a crash of glass, and then a rich gurgle of fluid, that sent a thrill of horror through my heart. Another crash, another gurgle, and then another and another, and even that strange scent of wine stronger and stronger. It must be as I thought, so I crept like a cat down the stairs once more, and gently opened the kitchen door. No one was there, but I heard another crash and my aunt's voice exclaim, in a tone of exalted fervour:—

"'Glory—Alleluia—another bait taken from Satan's trap!'

"I passed across the kitchen and looked through the door of the scullery, and there I saw my aunt and one of her red-cheeked servant wenches busily engaged in knocking the necks off the cobwebbed bottles and—oh, desecration!—pouring their priceless contents amid potato pairings, soapsuds, and beastliness of that sort down the sink to gladden the hearts of the rats in the main sewer.

"For a few moments, I was so taken aback I could not speak or move. It seemed like a ghostly dream. Yet it was real, and I could see an exalted look in my aunt's face, and as I heard her exclaim with each cruel decapitation, 'another bait snatched from Satan!' I knew the poor woman was earnest in her conviction, and I imagined she was doing right. As I looked at this strange scene, thinking what course to take, an exclamation behind me made me turn, and I saw in the kitchen the other red-cheeked servant girl, bearing on her muscular arm a bottle-basket holding a dozen of wine she had evidently brought up from the cellar for the purpose of immolation. O, William Slagg, you must have turned in your grave! If I had ever believed in ghosts, this work would have banished by belief, for if anything could have brought a ghost back to earth, the sacrifice going on would have brought yours back. That basket contained the very particular, the joy of your heart, the wine that only came forth on the most important occasions, the very opening of which was a religious ceremony, and fervent prayers went up over each bottle that the cork may have withstood the ravages of years and the wine be still sound! And now—

"Even if the servant had not discovered me, I should have interfered then, so I stepped boldly forwards into the scullery and confronted the heartless executioners. The servant, looking sheepish and ashamed, put down the bottle, the neck of which was just approaching the edge of the stone sink. My Aunt, with the consciousness of rectitude, met my gaze firmly.

"'Thank heaven I returned,' I said. 'What does this mean?'

"'Mean, John! Only that I am doing my duty.'

"'Doing your duty in pouring the finest cellar of wine in London down a common sink!'

"'You know my views, John. I say, touch not, taste not and handle not.'

"She has been touching and handling with a vengeance, I thought, but I kept my temper and said:—

"'But if you won't drink it, why not sell it and give the proceeds to the poor, if you like?'

"'No, John. I have considered the subject fully. My duty is to pour it down there. If I sell it—if I give it away—someone will drink, and every drop of wine that passes down a man's throat helps to float him to perdition.'

"Her imagery was strange, but her mind was made up, so, after a pause, I said:—

"'Come upstairs and talk with me. Tell your servants to stop for a bit.'

"She followed me, saying, 'It's no good talking, John; my mind is made up.'

"I cast about for a way to move her, and at last decided on a bold course.

"We seated ourselves in the dining-room, near that polished mahogany board in which poor old Uncle Slagg loved to see the crystal decanters mirrored.

"Then I commenced gravely—

"'My dear Aunt, you will understand that from motives of prudence I could not speak before your servants as I can now. Of course, I do not dispute your right to do what you like with your own, but I am sure you cannot be aware of the penalties you are incurring in this wholesale destruction of fermented liquors.'

"'How do you mean?' she said, startled.

"'I mean,' I replied, in the most solemn accents, 'that you are defrauding the excise and are liable to heavy fine and, I believe, imprisonment.'

"'But the wine is my own,' she argued.

"'Precisely; so is this sovereign mine, but were I to clip, debase or destroy it, I lay myself open to legal proceedings and punishment. Wine has paid duty and is protected in the same way as this sovereign.'

"'How unjust,' she said.

"'It may be so, but it is the law. Moreover, the informer gets a good share of the fine, so see how you place yourself in your servants' power and what temptation you expose them to.'

"'But I will go to prison and glory in my martyrdom,' she said, with an angelic look.

"'Excuse me, my dear Aunt, but I cannot afford to go to prison, and, as I am the executor and responsible for everything, I should share your fate. It may seem selfish, but I must guard against this. I shall, therefore, ask you to give me the key of the cellar; allow me to seal up the door, and I promise you, at the expiration of a twelvemonth, when I give you legal possession of everything here and take your discharge, I will return the key, and you must then please yourself.'

"Now, I well know how frightened women are at the idea of coming into collision with the law, so although the penalties I threatened her with were improbable and absurd, they set her thinking, and I awaited her answer hopefully. I added, though, as a make-weight:—

"'How terribly vexed poor uncle would have been to see you today.'

"'I believe, John, that in the place my poor husband now is, he fully realises the errors of his life, and could he look down'—or up I thought—'he would be pleased to see my actions.'

"I thought of the poor fellow as I last saw him at the table and smiled at the idea, but was too wise to contradict her. After a pause, she said:—

"'Well, John, you have been very kind and attentive, and I should not like you to get into trouble, so I will do as you wish. But, mind, at the end of twelve months nothing shall stop me throwing all the wine away.'

"I saw the basket of the 'very particular' safely restored to its snug bin; I locked the door, affixed my seal to it, and carried the key away; rejoicing that I had arrived in time to save the wine.

"But my task was not half over. I knew my Aunt so well, and felt sure she would carry out her threat at the expiration of the time named, so I wove a plot to obtain absolute possession of the wine, without putting her in a madhouse, or even forfeiting her goodwill or any chance legacy.

"I said not another word about the cellar, but, when the summer came, persuaded her to go away to the seaside for a short time. With all her magnificent conduct as to wasting alcoholic treasures, she was rather near, and said she could not afford it. She would like to go for a month or two, but found the expenses of her present house too great. I suggested letting it furnished for the time to a respectable tenant. She fell in with this suggestion, and when, through the house-agent, my friend Tom Sinclair offered to take the house at a handsome sum per week, and brought her unexceptional references, the matter was settled. Tom said he had his own servants, so she sent hers away on board wages. On the evening of the day she left, I met Tom by appointment at the house. His servants were all a myth, and there was no one to interfere with us. We broke the seal and opened the door, and found in the cellar, which had been excavated and enlarged by my old uncle's directions, at least five hundred bottles of wine, sleeping in beautifully-arranged bins, peacefully and happily, little dreaming how narrowly they had escaped total destruction.

"I determined to act with great caution. We had plenty of time before us, and I felt, to escape detection, the cellar must be left as we found it. I made an exact plan of it, marking the contents of the bins, and the number of bottles in each, and also noting the appearance as well I could. And then, Tom, commissioned by me, went round to auctioneers and wine merchants buying as cheaply as he could all the refuse he could find. Sour claret, fetid sherry, and fusty port formed the staple of his purchases. He was a perfect godsend to the lucky tradesmen he patronised, and if they ever imagined he was going to drink his purchases, all who sold him wine were equally guilty of manslaughter. We had it packed and sent to Tom's warehouse, and in two or three journeys hauled it to my Aunt's and stowed it in the basement. The house was in a quiet neighbourhood, and stood in a garden, so we ran little risk of detection. And then our work began. We were a month at it off and on, and I assure you the labour was so hard that only the thought of the rich reward enabled me to go through with it. We trusted no one, but did everything ourselves. We took the bins regularly, emptied them of their contents, unpacked a sufficient quantity of our dreadful purchases to replace them, and, having done that, filled the empty cases with the real Simon Pure[1], labelled each with the particulars, and nailed

---

[1] From the phrase 'the real Simon Pure', the name of a character in the play *A Bold Stroke for a Wife* (1717), by Susannah Centlivre (1669–1723), who is impersonated by another character in some scenes.

them down. In about a month our work was complete, and the five hundred and odd dozens of the old man's cherished wine lay ready packed for removal, whilst, through our carefulness, the cellar presented an appearance very much the same as it did before we commenced our meritorious task. The risk of detection was rendered less, from my Uncle having followed the old-fashioned plan of filling bins with sawdust. This, which was old and dirty, we carefully replaced, and, re-locking and re-sealing the door, after packing the last case, executed a dance of triumph at the success of our plot so far, and fully trusted to our cleverness in completely deceiving the old lady. In the dusk of the evening we sent two large wagons to the house, and by twelve o'clock that night the rescued treasures were safe in Tom's warehouse under lock and key. Of course, our operations had left the basement of my Aunt's house in a terrible litter, so we devoted another week to putting all that straight. This being done to our satisfaction, Tom wrote to Mrs. Slagg, and enclosed a cheque for two months' rent, saying that his plans being changed he intended to leave the house at once. The old lady, who had grown tired of the seaside, came back, and, although much disgusted at the dusty state she found the house in, and vowing nothing should induce her to let it again, never shows the slightest suspicion of what had transpired during her absence.

"Now that I was happy as to the wines, I waited with great curiosity to see whether, at the expiration of the time of probation, she would carry out her intentions. I found she was as firmly resolved as ever, and as I wished to see the end of the affair, after handing her the key, with a feigned protest, I told her I had almost persuaded myself with her ideas she could not do otherwise, and offered to give her any assistance I could in the good work. Almost incredulous, she accepted my aid, and a good work it was to pour the filthy contents of those bottles down the kitchen sink. Faugh! it nearly made us all sick; but I know my assistance on that occasion secures me a good legacy, as she altered her will in my favour the next day.

"The cream of the joke was that, as the servant girl brought up a basket full of the noxious compounds and reported that this was the very last, my Aunt hesitated for a few minutes, and, as perhaps some tender recollections of her late husband presented themselves, said to me:—

"'John, if you would like to take this last dozen, for your poor uncle's sake, you can. I ought to do away with all, I know, but one dozen is very little from the large quantity I have sacrificed. So take it, if you wish.'

"I trembled at the idea, and answered as one who overcomes a severe temptation:—

"'My dear Aunt, don't let any inclination of mine lead you from what you consider your duty. No doubt, I shall be better without it, so let it follow the rest.'

"She gave me a grateful smile, and the last dozen of William Slagg's supposed wine gurgled down the sink, and my aunt cleaned herself from the stains of the sacrifice, and went to a prayer meeting radiant and happy. She, no doubt, expects her reward hereafter, and doubtless she will receive it for if ever a good act was done in this world, she did one when she poured away that five hundred dozen of horrible stuff called wine."

John, having finished his tale, took a bright little key from his pocket, and rose.

"I suppose your friend Sinclair claimed some of the spoil?" I asked.

"Oh, yes, the wretch! Wanted a hundred and fifty dozen, but

I managed to compound for about half that quantity. So my cellar of wine was cheap after all, and I can well spare that other bottle I am now going to fetch."

THE END

At What Cost

It was late at night. The fire had gradually settled down until it became a steady, glowing mass of red, giving plenty of heat but little flame. The shaded lamp from the edge of the table threw a circle of light widening until it reached the floor, where it lay, a luminous disc, and left all outside in sombre gloom. The room was evidently a library, as tall cases of books loomed from each wall, and the massive table in the centre was strewn with pamphlets and writing materials. On a low chair near the fire, partly in light and partly in darkness, sat a woman. She might have been about forty-five years of age, and was still beautiful. Her hands, with the fingers interlaced, rested upon her lap and her head leant wearily against the side of the mantelpiece. Her attitude, even without the traces of recent tears upon her face, betokened extreme grief.

Well, indeed, might she grieve, for in the room above her lay a dead man—her husband. She had told her household to leave her and retire to rest, and hour after hour sounded as she sat by the fire and mourned in solitude.

True, the man who had died that day had not been her first love—not the one she had once hoped was destined to link his lot with hers. She had married him for esteem, friendship, respect, and many other admirable reasons, but her heart was with one who had died many years ago. Yet, they had been man and wife for twenty years, and his unwavering love, his kindness, the homage he had ever paid her, had earned, as with a woman they ever must, their reward; and as with sorrowful eyes she gazed into the fire and lived again those twenty placid years, she felt that Death had that day decreed a void in her life which would never again be filled.

And yet, the dead man had not been the most cheerful companion to a woman in the prime of health and beauty. He was ever sad, at times gloomy; but no harsh words to her had ever crossed his lips even in his most dreary moods. He had lived a fair and noble life, doing in a quiet, secret way much good in the place in which his life was spent; good the extent of which she, perhaps, only knew. And as she thought of these things, and of the poor white face upstairs, another flood of tears came to her relief. She would see it once more to-night, and, by the side of that motionless form, kneel down and say, "If I have not loved you as your heart wished, I have done all that I could—all that I promised." With this intention she rose from her seat, and rising, an object on the mantelpiece attracted her attention. It was a small key, and that morning, even as he died, her husband, with feeble fingers, had placed it in her hand, whispering with a yearning look on his wan face, "Read and forgive."

In the agitation of that terrible hour, she had taken little notice of those mysterious words—the last, indeed, he spoke—but now she remembered them, and felt there was something he wished her to know.

The key, she was aware, gave access to a secretaire in which her husband kept his private papers. She raised the shade from the lamp, and its light hitherto concentrated, spread over and illuminated the room, in one corner which stood a black walnut bureau, with antique brass handles. She opened it, and, after a few moments' search, found what she intuitively knew was the document designed for her perusal. It was a bulky packet, sealed and addressed: "For my Wife; Private."

Wondering, even in her grief, what its contents could possibly be, and why the instructions to read it were coupled with that piteous appeal for forgiveness, she returned to her former seat, and, after adjusting the light, broke open the seals and commenced the perusal of the manuscript. Woman-like, she turned over several pages rapidly, as if to catch some idea of the general tenour of the revelation; and, as in the cursory glance she took, she saw one name, a well-known name, written frequently, a feeling of fear thrilled her, and, with a low cry of pain and horror, she set her lips firmly, and, with eager eyes, devoured the closely-written lines. The message from the man who lay dead ran thus:

* * *

My Wife,

When you read this I shall be dead, and you will, I have little doubt, be still in the prime of womanhood. Whether the love I have ever borne you, whether the remembrance of those years spent, at least happily, under this roof together, will enable you after reading this to think of me without cursing my name, I know not. Yet, I dare not die and make no sign. I dare not let the grave cover the secret which is fretting my life out—which has twined for years around my heart like a snake, and which will, at last, still its beating—a secret that even you in your wildest dreams never suspected.

As you read these pages you will weep, but not for me. You will call for one who can never return, but the name you utter will not be mine. Widowed though you be, it is not your husband you will mourn. Yet, when this is written, my mind will be more at ease, although I know the confession which may lighten my remorse a little, lays a heavy burden on you. At least forgive me this.

How shall I begin? As I sit here tonight, a prematurely aged man, I look back through the long years—so long, so weary to me—and see myself in this same room, a young man of twenty five, with all that could make life pleasant at my command, riches and friends—youth and health—and, as I fondly hoped at that time, love that, sooner or later, would be mine. Here I sat, I remember, one winter's evening, with my favourite companions even then—my books. Was I reading, or was I dreaming of what might be? I know not.

My servant entered and handed me a card—*Mr Gerald Gordon*—I shall feel, even in my grave, your heart throb as you read that name. Gerald Gordon had been one of my earliest and dearest friends; and, if I lost sight of this for some years, never forgotten. I was delighted to find him under my roof, and hastened to greet him. He had prospered in the world, both having made and inherited money, and recently returned to England after some years' profitable work abroad. Affairs had called him to my neighbourhood, and upon his return journey he had come a little out of his way to pay me a visit for the sake of old times.

We were unfeignedly glad to meet, and, as our hands clasped, many recollections of happy, boyish days rose between us, and the pressing invitation I gave him to stay some time with me was accepted as freely and heartily as it was given.

For you, Gertrude, least of all, need I paint his portrait; but well I remember as he sat with me that night, looking at his handsome face, with those straight, clear-cut features, bronzed by the southern sun; his crisp, brown hair, and stalwart, manly frame, and thinking one of the greatest gifts, after all, was personal appearance.

Our conversation after so long a separation naturally consisted of questions and answers of a personal nature, and I soon asked him:

"Have you met your fate yet, Gerald?"

"Been in love, I suppose you mean?" he replied, laughing. "Well, you see, I have just come from parts where a fellow must make love, or pretend to, to get along at all; but I cannot plead guilty to any grand passion as yet.

"But how about you?" he continued. "Have any bright rustic eyes come between you and your books?"

Fool that I was not to open my heart to him then and there! Not to tell him I thought of one woman only! Yet, I was shy and proud. I could not even say that my love was viewed favourably. A withered flower, given half in jest—do you remember it? A little preference, it might be, over my rivals, and that bestowed for the sake of friendship, not love—this was all I had to show in return for the love I had given and which I knew must ever give through life. So I laughed as he questioned me, and answered as in jest:

"I am heart-whole as you, Gerald, and certainly invulnerable against the attacks of rustic maidens hereabouts."

"I hoped and expected to be introduced to your future wife in the person of the only daughter of some neighbouring squire; and would have done you a good turn by sounding your praises whilst I admired his fat oxen."

"Well, I will present you to all the eligible daughters hereabout, and you can praise their papa's oxen on your own account."

"Thank you—although, seriously, I am tired of living alone and want a wife and a home; so I am quite ready to meet my fate when and wherever she appears."

I do not hesitate, my wife, to record these trivial words, for I know they will seem to you as sweet echoes of a long-stilled voice.

Gordon and I sat talking nearly all that night, and parted, at last, each happy to find the other's friendship the same as of old.

The next day, with little regret, I tossed my books aside and did all in my power to make my guest's visit a pleasant one to him. We shot, drove, and rode together, and the short wintry days seemed even shorter with my light-hearted friend at my side. I took him to visit all my friends save one; I need scarcely say the reason for that omission. Too well I knew that, had I been a girl, Gerald Gordon was the man who might have won my heart had he chosen. Too well I knew that, if the eyes of love enhanced, they did not imagine your charms, and that his interest, at least, could scarcely fail to be aroused. So I dreaded to bring about a meeting between him and you. It came at last. I would have shunned that gathering could I have found a decent pretext, but the whole countryside were bidden to that ball, and my absence from it would have been remarked. Besides, Gerald would have gone anyway. He was very merry as we drove over, at the expense of the imaginary persons we should meet; but I said nothing. The moment we entered the room I saw his eyes fall upon you. I saw his look of surprise, of admiration, as he comprehended your regal beauty at one glance, and, before the evening was over, I felt that what I dreaded was afoot, and that my friend would probably be my rival. If his attentions to you that evening were no more than man might properly pay to the most attractive woman in the assemblage, they were sufficient to make me feel the worst. Even as I write this, I can see his tall figure bending over you, and hear him whispering words which, spoken with the easy, self-confident manners of a man of the world, I knew intuitively must have been sweet to any young girl's ears.

At last that night, gay and enjoyable to all save me, ended. You had departed, and after that it needed little persuasion on my part to draw Gerald from the scene. We started on our drive home, with the stars shining pure and clear through the frosty skies. I was sullen and unhappy; my companion brimful of curiosity to learn all I could tell him concerning his late partner.

"Is Miss Howard a friend of yours?" was his first question.

"I have known her some years. Do you admire her? Although I need to scarcely ask," I added, bitterly.

"Admire her! I should think so. I have seen some of the most beautiful women in the world, but never one I admired more. She was not very well dressed, of course, but that is only a milliner's business."

So he talked on and on as we drove that six miles of road, and my heart sank within me, and I cursed the friendship which had led him to visit me and introduced me to press him to prolong his stay. He spoke of nothing but you, ringing your praises in various keys, until I relapsed into a sort of moody silence, or only answered his eulogistic remarks by monosyllables. Probably he noticed my changed manner, as, on reaching home, he said:

"You are awfully tired, I can see, Philip; so I will be merciful tonight and not keep you up for another cigar. Good night."

Whether he kept me up or not, it mattered nothing. Weary as I truly was, there was little sleep for me that night.

When we met the next morning it was the same again, your image clearly was before his eyes. Although he spoke jestingly of the havoc you had wrought, I knew that more than jest lay under the laughing exterior; that the impression you had made was no transient one. I tried to hide my feelings, and to answer his playful remarks in the like vein, but my efforts were of little use. I felt that his keen eye detected something amiss with me. He looked inquisitive, but said nothing for a while. After breakfast, as we were discussing our plans for the day, he asked:

"Would it not be politeness to ride over and enquire how Miss Howard is after last night's dissipation?"

I started, and answered, "If you wish it particularly we will do so"; and, as I forced the words, my voice sounded strange and I felt that the colour had left my cheeks.

The manner of my assent must, I suppose, have strengthened any suspicion he already felt as to the truth as to the true state of the case with me, for he crossed the room, placed his hands on my shoulders, and with his bright, searching eyes looked deep into mine.

"Tell me truly, Philip—truly, mind—is there anything like love between you two?"

Even then I might have told him, but I was too proud to say I loved without love in return. Too proud to throw myself on his mercy, as it seemed to me such a confession must; so I met his eyes without quailing, and answered firmly:

"There is no love between us."

"But you do love her?" persisted Gerald.

"I admire her for her great beauty; that is all."

And even as I told the lie, I saw that he believed what he wished to believe, and I knew that my fate was sealed.

"Then let us go," he said, quietly, as he moved his hands from my shoulders.

We rode over to your home; we saw you, and my jealous eyes detected a faint blush and look of pleasure on your face as you greeted us—a blush and a look such as my coming alone had never yet called forth.

Gertrude, it is for you, not for me, to picture the events of the next few days. Sick at heart, I pleaded indisposition and returned to my books; sacrificing politeness, I left Gordon free to follow his own devices. Well did I know whither his steps turned every day, and clearly could I read in the brightened expression of his ever bright face how well the suit he was urging prospered. So much so, that it was with a feeling of dull despair, not surprise, I listened when one night he told me you had consented to be his wife. Lover-like, he sat hour after hour dilating upon the perfections of the prize he had won, and revelling in his visions of future happiness. And I, who loved you as I believe no man ever yet loved a woman, suffered torture on the rack of his raptures. I had to listen to your praises from the lips of the one whom I had now almost brought myself to believe had robbed me of all I longed for in the world. And there was to be no delay—no respite for me. He was wealthy, so what was there to wait for? Within three months' time you were to be married.

"How I bless the day I came to see you, old fellow," he cried once in the effusion of his joy. "Now you shall complete your kindness by letting me stay with you until the happy time. Of course, I must go away for a bit to see about a house and that sort of thing, but I mean to be here as much as I can."

If I had followed my true impulse as he spoke, I should have cursed him and bade him begone; but I was forced to restrain myself and tell him how welcome he was to make my house his home as long as it pleased him. Yet, I felt I did not stay myself and witness his happiness. That night, as I lay in bed casting about for an excuse plausible enough to enable me to leave my guest alone for the next month or two, I knew that in the depths of my heart I hated Gerald Gordon—I hated him as the one who had stolen my life's hope from me—I hated him for his animal spirits, his good looks, his power of pleasing and winning the affection of man, woman, or child; so different from me—I even hated him because I knew you would be happy with him, for he had all the qualities to make a home happy—I hated him as Cain hated Abel, and for the same reason: had not his offering been accepted and mine rejected? And several days passed by; each day the tortures I endured seemed greater; each day my hatred grew more intense. In a feverish sort of way I forced myself to laugh and jest, and Gordon, with a lover's selfishness, never noticed now how unnatural my manner was, or guessed how by this time, I detested the sound of his voice, the clear ring of his laugh, or even his very presence.

"One thing pleases me more than I can say," he placidly remarked one evening. "It is that what I once believed to be a fact was only a creation of my own brain. I was afraid I might be the rival of my old friend; but Gertrude herself assures me the only feeling that ever existed between you two was one of pure friendship. So I am happier, knowing that you will dance at my wedding with a light heart."

Dance at the wedding! I would rather dance on my mother's grave!

* * *

Gertrude, my wife, there is one day in every year which is solemn and sad to both of us. A day when the choicest flowers are laid on a tomb now growing grey with time. A day, many hours of which you spend alone, holding a lock of hair and gazing on a miniature. And yet, if the love you bore another man is strong in your heart, upon that day you have ever seemed to draw closer to me than at other times. As your eyes, sideways unforgotten sorrow, meet mine, you think, 'Our grief is from the same source—mine for love and his for friendship.' And with one memory between us, I know for the moment your heart grows nearer to mine, and I realise what life might have been could your love have crowned it. Read now the truth and hate me.

That day was the first for a long time I had spent alone with Gerald Gordon. You were away on a visit to some friends at a distance. The weather was fine, though wintry, and as I felt I could not enjoy the long hours indoors, in the society of the man I hated, I suggested taking our guns and walking down to the coast in the hope of shooting some ducks. Gordon leapt at the idea. "I shall be glad to do a bit of hard walking," he said; "for three weeks I have only been love-making, and that isn't much exercise. I fancy my muscles must be growing soft from want of using."

As he spoke he held out an arm like an iron bar for me to feel.

An hour's walk brought us to the coast; you know it well. For the distance of perhaps two miles, runs a turf-covered, almost perpendicular cliff; then it shelves away gradually, and one can easily get down to the water's edge. Here was our destination. We intended to walk along the edge of the sea, shooting anything worth powder and shot.

The tide, when high, lashes the foot of the coast cliff; when low, it leaves a strip of sand uncovered. The rock of which the cliff is composed is of crumbling, unstable chalk, and has the habit of getting hollowed out under the surface, leaving green cushions, firm enough in appearance, but apt to break away as the unwary foot presses on them. A dangerous cliff it is, from the edge of which one shrinks instinctively.

We walked briskly along the greensward; I was some paces in front of Gordon, not being much in the humour to listen to his inevitable rhapsodies on the one theme. As he followed, I could hear him singing a love song. It was Mexican, I believe, and picked up somewhere on his travels. Though the language was strange to me, the words sounded soft and musical, and the repetition of the passionate refrain almost maddened me, so well did I know to whom it was directed. Suddenly, the melody of the song changed to a sharp cry of despair—a cry that went through me like a knife—and, as I turned hastily round, the rent at the edge of the treacherous greensward told its tale, even before I heard the horrible, hopeless, dull thud on the sand below.

Believe me, when I say, at that moment all thought of hatred and envy left me. Horror-stricken, I threw myself at full length on the grass and crept to the edge of the cliff, looking for what I dreaded to see—his mangled body. The cliff at this spot overhung even more than usual, and it was with a feeling of hope I saw that Gordon had fallen clear of the rock and lay upon the sand. He was lying almost in a heap, and must have sustained fearful injuries; but dead he was not, for I saw him, after making a few piteous struggles, succeed in turning his face towards me.

"Gerald," I cried, "are you much hurt? For God's sake try and answer me."

A faint voice—the ghost of his usual voice—replied: "I have broken one arm and, I think, my thigh. Can you come down to me?"

"I cannot," I said, "without going along the coast for a mile or more. I am going now to get ropes and help. Try and bear up till I return."

And then, leaving my gun to mark the spot where he fell, I turned, and, swiftly as I could, commenced running across country. I knew the part well. The nearest house was at least two miles away, so the poor fellow must lie in agony for some time before I could bring him the indispensable aid. With the remembrance of that helpless form lying on the sand before me, my thoughts were only how to rescue him with as little loss of time as possible, and for the first five minutes I ran at the top of my speed. Sheer exhaustion then compelled me to pause and draw breath, and, as I moderated my pace, the awful thought for the first time came to me. The tide! The tide! I remembered it was rising—that it was about three-quarters flood—that Gordon was lying very near to the edge of the water, and I knew if I could not bear him aid before the sea covered that narrow strip of sand he was a dead man. And then the temptation began. Let no man say there is no devil, but I tell you in that moment the devil was with me! He brought your form, with all its beauty, before me; yes, and with love for me shining in your eyes. He shaped the thought in my mind, 'It is for her, who might love you, you are saving him. Is she not worth the sin?' And, as the tempter prompted me, I said to myself, 'One half hour's delay; a rest by the way; a fancied inability to proceed further; a mistake—so easy to make—in the road, and you are free once more and may yet be mine.' The price was crime—loss of honour, of self-respect, and all peace of mind; but, you might be mine, and what price was too heavy to pay for that? And, as thought after thought, each like a devil from hell, came to me, I leant against the gate, knowing as I did so that every moment I lingered risked a man's life. The sudden temptation, the commencement of the crime, the consequences to follow, the shame I felt, even then, bewildered me, and for a time I was beside myself. I seemed in a dream; all around me was unreal; the air seemed full of horrible forms and sounds. How long I waited motionless I cannot tell—would that I knew!—it might have been moments, minutes, or hours. At last, it seemed as though I woke, and, as I turned and ran like one pursued by wolves, I fancied I heard the words, 'Too late! Too late!' shrieked after me in fiendish glee. As I ran, I believe I even ceased to think, and fell utterly exhausted at the door of the farmhouse, to which I mechanically directed my steps. In broken sentences I told my tale; I begged the men to hurry down with ropes; I offered large rewards should they reach the coast in time to avert what I now shuddered to think might happen. They started with all possible despatch, and, as soon as my strength returned to me, I followed. Gertrude, how can I pen the rest? I reached the fatal spot just as the men from the farm lowered one of their party over the edge of the cliff, and, as sick and dizzy I leant over, I saw beneath me the cruel waves—in a dark form against the crueller rocks; and, as one of the men turned to me and said, "Poor chap; if we had been a quarter of an hour sooner we might have saved him," I knew that in the eye of God I was as much a murderer as the ruffian who drives a knife through the heart of his victim. Little wonder was it, as they bore his nerveless form to the top of the cliff, as I saw the pale face, stained here and there with blood, the blue eyes yet open, and, as I almost fancied, seeking my own, that I fell as one dead upon the grass, and was borne away unconscious as the man I had foully slain.

What more remains to be said? You know the rest—how the illness that followed was attributed to the shock I had undergone and the exertions I had used to save my friend; how people praised my presence of mind in at once starting for assistance; how you—even you—wrote kind words to me—words that cut my heart like knives. Yet, no one knew that with me, night and day, was the face of the dead, as I saw it ere I fell senseless on the cliff; that ever in my dreams I was running, it seemed to be, from an image of you, and that fearful things were striving to stop me. No one knew how often I went to the spot where Gordon fell, and timed, as nearly as I could, the rising waters, to ascertain if it were possible for a man to have compassed the distance and brought aid in time to save him. Alas, I only learnt I was a murderer in act as well as thought! I gained the prize that tempted me—but at what a cost! When, after some years, you gave me your hand, I knew your heart could never be mine, but lay in Gerald's grave; I knew that the thing which at last induced you to accede to my repeated request was more the love you fancied I bore him than the love you felt for me. And so, at the price of a life's remorse, I won a woman whose love in life could never be mine, and who, after death, must hate my memory.

Ah, Gerald Gordon, slain by the waves at the bidding of your friend, just as the supreme joy of life was yours, your lot, after all, was happier than mine!

***

As she read the last words, Gertrude Blake dropped the manuscript, and, burying her face in her hands, cried, "O! why did he tell me? Why did he tell me? This is the worst of all to bear. Thank God I have no children in whose faces I may see 'Murderer' written." Then, with bitter grief and hatred in her heart, she sat on and on through the weary night. And ever before her was the image of Gerald Gordon, with the hungry waters creeping round him, his poor maimed limbs battling in vain struggles to keep his life until the delayed help arrived. And her face was stern and cold as she pictured it. If her husband's hopes of heaven rested on her forgiveness, she felt she could not bring her lips to frame the words.

She could scarcely credit the tale she had read; at times she fancied it must have been in a great part imagination. But his face, ever sad, and even when others were gayest, came again and again to her mind, and she felt that strange sadness stamped the confession with truth. Yet, in all else, he had been so noble, both in thought and deed. He had loved her so; and now, with his dreary secret bared before her, even through the bitterness of her mind passed the knowledge that he had been leading not only a life of remorse, but also of atonement, and, as she grew more calm, she fell at last into a troubled sleep with wet tears upon her lashes.

And as she slept, she dreamed. They stood before her, she thought: her first and only love, Gerald, and her husband. The latter, not the careworn, prematurely old man of past years, but young, gay and handsome as when he rode with Gerald to see her that morning in the winter. There was no sadness in his eyes now, and Gerald's arm was round his neck:—"Sweet love," she heard him whisper, "see, I have forgiven—cannot you likewise?" And then, striving to speak, she awoke.

With the dream yet lingering in her memory, she rose, and tearing the manuscript to shreds, threw it upon the smouldering fire. When every vestige of paper was consumed, she sought her room, but, as she passed the chamber of death she entered, and, bending over the pale, cold, placid face, kissed it, whispering: "I forgive, as I hope to be forgiven."

THE END

VERY SHORT CLASSICS

This book is part of the 'Very Short Classics' series, a collection of short books from around the world and across the centuries, many of which are being made available as ebooks, and paperbacks, for the very first time.

Also available in the Very Short Classics series...

THE FOUR DEVILS by Herman Bang

A classic of Danish literature.

When their mother drowns, young brothers Fritz and Adolf are sold into the circus by their grandmother, for a mere twenty marks. There they suffer under the cruel hand of Father Cecchi but are befriended by sisters Aimée and Louise and together they create an acrobatic act.

When Cecchi dies and the circus disbands, the quartet find there is little demand for acrobats and they refine their skills, re-emerging as The Four Devils, death-defying trapeze artists. Soon they are the talk of Europe, flying high from one city to another.

But one of the Four Devils, Aimée, finds that her feelings

for Fritz have outgrown that of a sibling love and become a passion that pervades her every waking moment. So when Fritz begins an affair with an aristocratic heiress, Aimée's heart is broken and tensions threaten to also break the Four Devils apart, forever.

The Four Devils is a short novella from one of Denmark's most acclaimed writers.

SOUVENIRS OF FRANCE by Rudyard Kipling

'Sixty pages... of memory, praise, nostalgia and gratitude'
Julian Barnes

Rudyard Kipling's love affair with India is well-documented but his affection for France and its people is less well-known. It started at the age of twelve when he would regularly accompany his father to the Paris Exhibition of 1878, where the elder Kipling was in charge of the Indian Section of Arts and Manufactures. Young Rudyard would be sent off in the morning with two francs in his pocket and instructions to stay out of trouble. He would spend his money on 'satisfying déjeuners' and 'celestial gingerbreads' as well as frequent trips up inside the head of the Statue of Liberty, then part of the Exhibition prior to being shipped to Ellis Island.

He returned to France a decade later, as a young man, and then regularly in the years that followed, sometimes for pleasure, sometimes on business – such as when working for the British Imperial War Graves Commission. He was a frequent visitor for the rest of his life.

Souvenirs of France was originally published in 1933, and was one of the last of Kipling's books to appear during his lifetime. It is a very personal and fascinating portrait of a great writer and of a country that had a special place in his heart.

CHILDLESS by Ignát Herrmann

A classic Czech novella.

When Ivan Hron is expelled from university because of his political beliefs he is kicked out of the family home and disinherited by his father. He finds a job in Prague as a bank clerk, works hard and impresses his employers. Some years later, he is appointed manager.

Now a man of considerable means he is keen to get married and start a family. One summer holiday he meets Magdalena, a young woman from the country who is at the resort with her parents, and falls in love. But his proposal of marriage is refused.

Six months pass and Ivan hears that Magda's father has fallen upon hard times. He gets back in touch, repeats his proposal and this time is accepted. And although their union is seemingly a happy one, it remains childless, much to Ivan's distress.

One day, Ivan discovers a letter his wife has hidden from him. The contents shatter his illusions of their happy marriage and reveal secrets that challenge everything he has hoped for in life.

But his reaction will surprise those around him and, quite possibly, the reader too.

Childless is a short novella by a revered Czech writer whose work is little-known in English. Its forward-thinking philosophy, way ahead of its time, makes it a story that deserves a modern readership.

This edition first published by Very Short Classics 2019

Copyright © Very Short Classics 2019

All rights reserved. No part of this publication may be reproduced, stored or transmitted in any form or by any means, electronic, mechanical, photocopying, recording, scanning, or otherwise without written permission from the publisher. It is illegal to copy this book, post it to a website, or distribute it by any other means without permission.

Originally published by John and Robert Maxwell in 1885.

This book was professionally typeset on Reedsy. Find out more at reedsy.com

ISBN: 979-8655360099

Printed in Poland
by Amazon Fulfillment
Poland Sp. z o.o., Wrocław